Clean it!

illustrated by Georgie Birkett

Child's Play (International) Ltd
Swindon   Auburn ME   Sydney
Illustration © 2009 G. Birkett   ISBN 978-1-84643-283-5
© 2009 Child's Play (International) Ltd   Printed in China
1 3 5 7 9 10 8 6 4 2
www.childs-play.com

Let's make the beds. Where's the pillow?

I'm all tangled up! Where's my teddy?

What a lot of laundry! I'm in my boat.

Hang this one up next. Is Teddy dry yet?

Is the laundry dry? Shall we fold it up?

Do these match? How many pairs are there?

What needs ironing? Please can I help?

Which drawer do these go in? Next please!

We have to clear up! My toys go in here.

I can reach the ball. Where's my teddy?

What can you see in the mirror now it's clean?

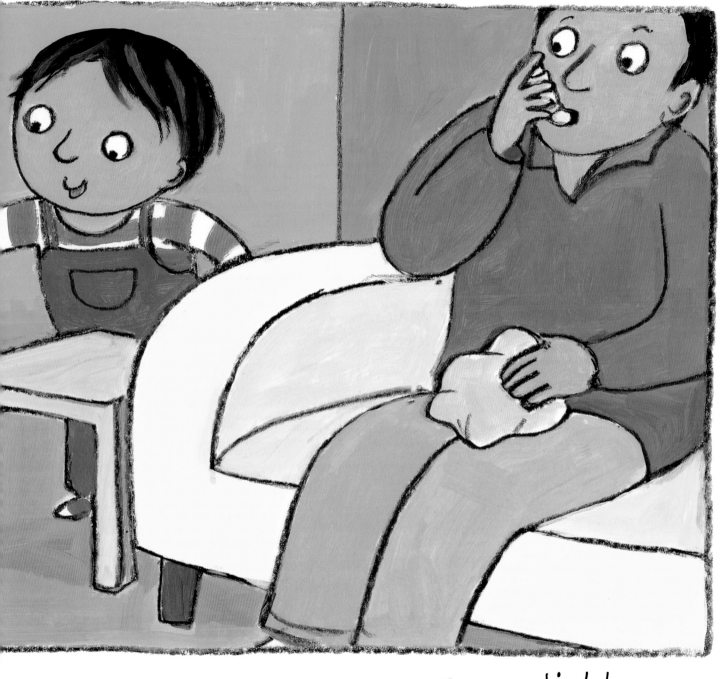

How far can this reach? I can tickle you!

This is my book! Look what I've found!

Oh no! What's happening? Poor Doggy!

I've nearly finished. Is there any more?

It's all clean now. Who'll dry my tea set?

All these need sorting. Where does this go?

Is there any more paper? This is nearly full.

All done! This sink is sparkling clean!

Can I rinse the bath? Whoops! You're wet!

Look at all this mess. Shall I sweep it up?

Don't drink that! And no muddy paws!

Time for a rest. Oh no! Not more mess!